STELLA
and the
SEAGULL

OXFORD
UNIVERSITY PRESS

Great Clarendon Street, Oxford OX2 6DP
Oxford University Press is a department of the University of Oxford.
It furthers the University's objective of excellence in research, scholarship,
and education by publishing worldwide. Oxford is a registered trade mark of
Oxford University Press in the UK and in certain other countries

Text copyright © Georgina Stevens 2020
Illustrations © Izzy Burton 2020
The moral rights of the author and illustrator have been asserted
Database right Oxford University Press (maker)
First published 2020

British Library Cataloguing in Publication Data

Data available
ISBN: 978-0-19-277468-2

1 3 5 7 9 10 8 6 4 2

Printed in China

Paper used in the production of this book is a natural,
recyclable product made from wood grown in sustainable forests.
The manufacturing process conforms to the environmental
regulations of the country of origin.

Georgina Stevens · Izzy Burton

STELLA
and the
SEAGULL

OXFORD
UNIVERSITY PRESS

Stella loved living with Granny Maggie by the sea.

They were not allowed to **keep** pets, but they did have one regular little visitor…

'What have you found for me today,
little seagull?'

It was always the highlight of
Stella's day when her little friend
came to visit.

At first, Stella loved the gifts
she brought with her.

But lately, it was
all plastic straws,
balloons, bottle
tops . . .

. . . and wrappers.

'That's my favourite chocolate bar!' laughed Stella. 'Just a shame someone else has eaten the chocolate!'

But one day, the little seagull
did not appear at all.

'Perhaps we should go and look for her,
Granny Maggie,' suggested Stella.

When they spotted her on the beach,
Stella knew she was poorly.

'We should take her to the vets,' said
Granny Maggie, 'straight away.'

The vet was very worried
about the little seagull.

'Your little friend has eaten a lot of plastic. I will need to take it all out and keep her here for a few days to help her get better.'

Stella wished that she could help the little seagull herself, but she knew she needed to stay with the vet.

On the way home, Stella could not stop thinking about her little friend.

'This must be where she found all of the plastic,' said Stella.

'Maybe if we pick some of it up now, it will stop other animals getting poorly too?'

So Stella and Granny Maggie started picking
up some of the litter around them . . .

Though they soon realised there was just too much for them to manage.

Until a poster gave Stella an idea ...

BRAMPTON SANDS

SUMMER SOLSTICE BEACH PARTY

THIS WEEKEND!

'We should have a Beach Clean Party!' Stella exclaimed.
'See if anyone wants to come and help!'

'I'm sure they will,'
said Granny Maggie.
'Especially if we
make a cake too.'

When they got home, they set to
work making a poster for the party.

What a lovely poster it was!

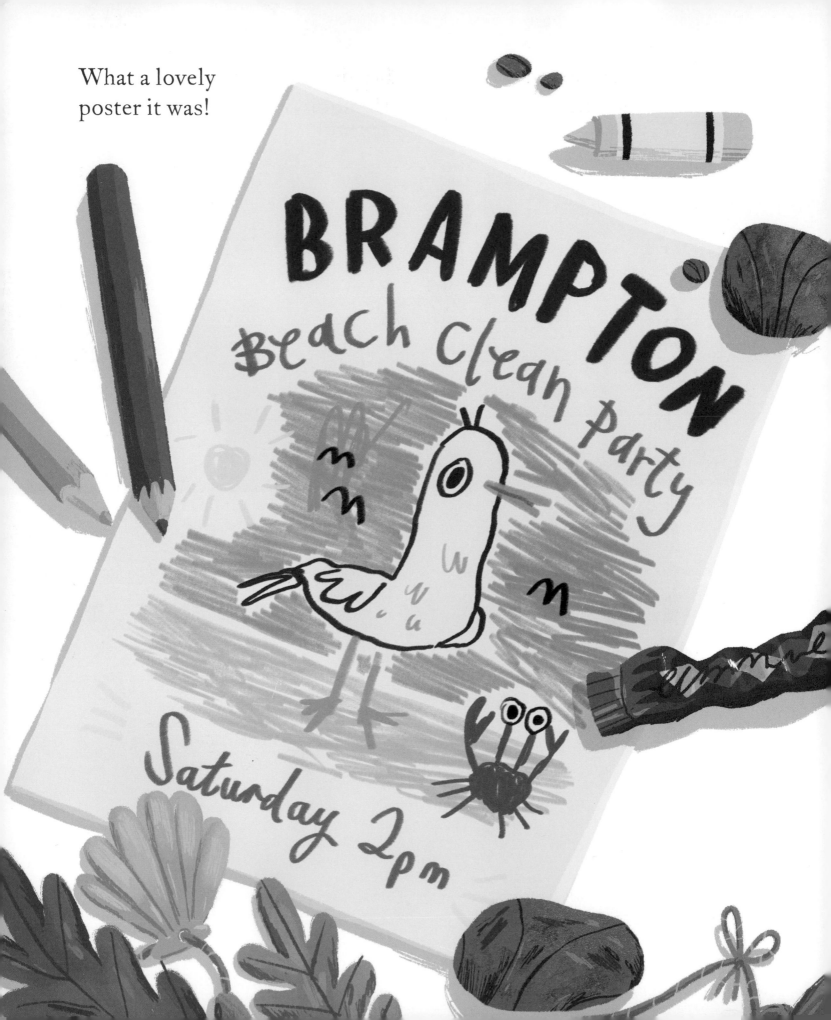

The next day, Granny Maggie and Stella
took their poster to all of the shops in town.

Everyone was very sad
to hear the story about
the little seagull, and
wanted to help.

Soon the posters for the beach clean
party started appearing everywhere!

Back at their flat, Stella still couldn't stop thinking about the little seagull.

And then she spotted something on one of the wrappers . . .

'Look Granny Maggie! Here is the chocolate company's address.

Maybe if we write to them, they might be able to help?'

And so Granny Maggie helped Stella
to write them a letter . . .

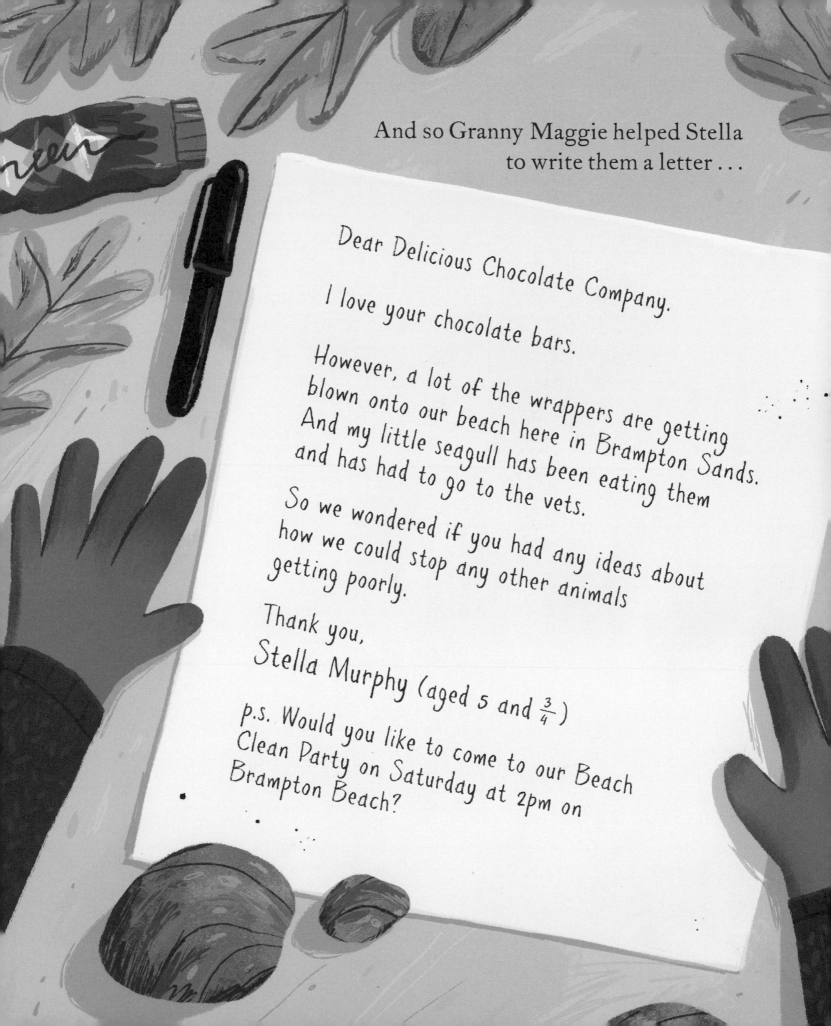

Dear Delicious Chocolate Company.

I love your chocolate bars.

However, a lot of the wrappers are getting blown onto our beach here in Brampton Sands. And my little seagull has been eating them and has had to go to the vets.

So we wondered if you had any ideas about how we could stop any other animals getting poorly.

Thank you,
Stella Murphy (aged 5 and $\frac{3}{4}$)

p.s. Would you like to come to our Beach Clean Party on Saturday at 2pm on Brampton Beach?

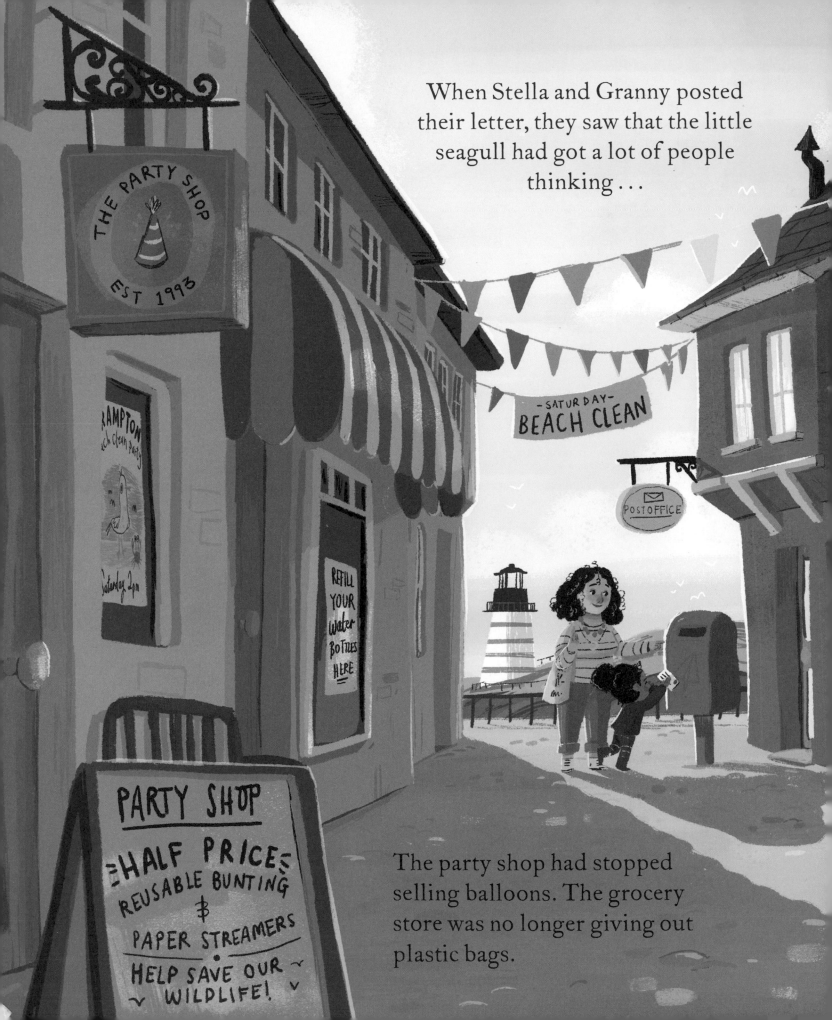

When Stella and Granny posted their letter, they saw that the little seagull had got a lot of people thinking . . .

The party shop had stopped selling balloons. The grocery store was no longer giving out plastic bags.

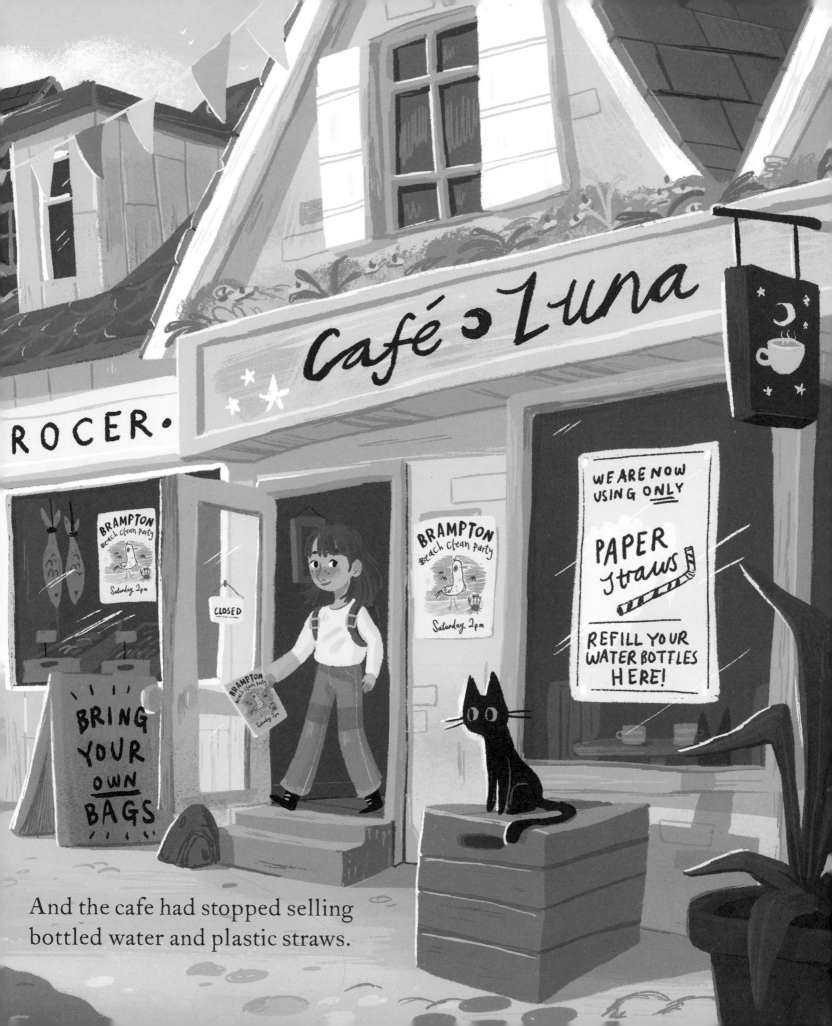

And the cafe had stopped selling
bottled water and plastic straws.

And more good news came when Stella got a letter back from the Delicious Chocolate Company.

Dear Ms Stella Murphy,

Thank you so much for your letter.

We are so happy that you like our chocolate bars, but we are very sorry to hear that our wrappers are littering your beach, and that your little seagull is poorly.

We have an idea as to how we can help. But perhaps we could start by coming to your beach clean party and giving out chocolate, without the wrappers, to everyone who has come to help.

All best wishes,

Ms Divine Angelou,
CEO Delicious Chocolate

'My favourite chocolate bar has just got even better!'
said Stella. 'But I do hope lots of people come to
help on Saturday. We won't be able to clean the
whole beach ourselves.'

But Stella needn't have worried!
EVERYONE who had heard about
the little seagull came out to help!

'I think our little seagull would be really proud of us,' said Stella.

'Me too,' replied Granny Maggie, 'if only she could be here to see it . . .'

Then the best news of all . . .
'Look, Granny Maggie,'
said Stella. 'The little seagull
is here!'

Thanks to the vet, the little
seagull was feeling much better.

The two friends were so happy to see each other again and to be back on the beach—especially now that it was clean.

When all of the plastic was sorted out for recycling, the celebrations started . . .

What a *wonderful* party it was!

From then on, the little seagull brought Stella much less plastic from the beach.

But when she did, Stella found a very good use for it.

PLEASE KEEP OUR BEACH

PLASTIC FREE!

SWAP WRAPPERS FOR CHOCOLATE

And the chocolate company had found a very good way to recycle their old wrappers too . . .

BRAMPTON BEACH PLAY PARK

MADE FROM RECYCLED CHOCOLATE WRAPPERS

FILL UP HERE

THE FACTS BEHIND THE STORY

- More than 9 out of 10 seabirds have eaten plastic, which sits in their tummies and can stop them eating unless it is removed quickly.

- Helium balloons are not recyclable and if released can injure or be eaten by animals or birds. Reusable bunting and paper streamers are much cooler!

- Bottle tops are easily eaten by many animals, and are largely unrecyclable. Try to avoid using single-use water bottles, and use any bottle tops for your own art project, like Stella did.

- Our food often comes in unrecyclable plastic packaging which ends up in landfill or in the sea. Why not ask your local supermarket if they will take back or change some of their packaging?

- Our old plastic can be made into all sorts of things such as playgrounds, clothes and surfboards. This is great, but we still need to use less single-use plastic because only a small amount is recycled. Do you think you could use fewer pieces of new plastic? You will be helping to keep our amazing planet healthier for everyone.

Many young people around the world are raising awareness of PLASTIC and making change happen . . .

5-year-old Ava James wrote to her favourite pizza restaurant asking them to stop using PLASTIC STRAWS, as she had heard that they can hurt turtles. The company removed them from all of its restaurants within 6 months.

Charlie Hamilton-Cooper started doing beach clean ups when he was 4 and has cleaned over 50 beaches so far.

A group of school children did not want their milk served in a PLASTIC carton with a PLASTIC STRAW, so they asked their school to serve their milk in REUSABLE beakers instead. Could you get your school to cut its use of PLASTIC?

Every Friday, Greta Thunberg and many young people around the world have been gathering outside town halls to ask governments to support our environment. Perhaps you could write to your local councillor with some ideas about how they could make things better.

GEORGINA STEVENS is a sustainability advisor, writer and campaigner. She advises organisations and individuals on how they can have significant positive impact on our planet. She also organises the Be The Change events to help people realise the power we all have to affect major change. And when she's not writing, you can find her forest bathing or planting things.

www.georginastevens.org

IZZY BURTON is a film director and artist. She makes short films, children's books and adverts, and produces designs for the television and film industries. On her rare days off, you'll find her watching Star Wars, drinking Earl Grey tea (no milk, lemon if there is some) and concocting elaborate plans on how she can feasibly have a dog in her life.

www.izzyburton.co.uk